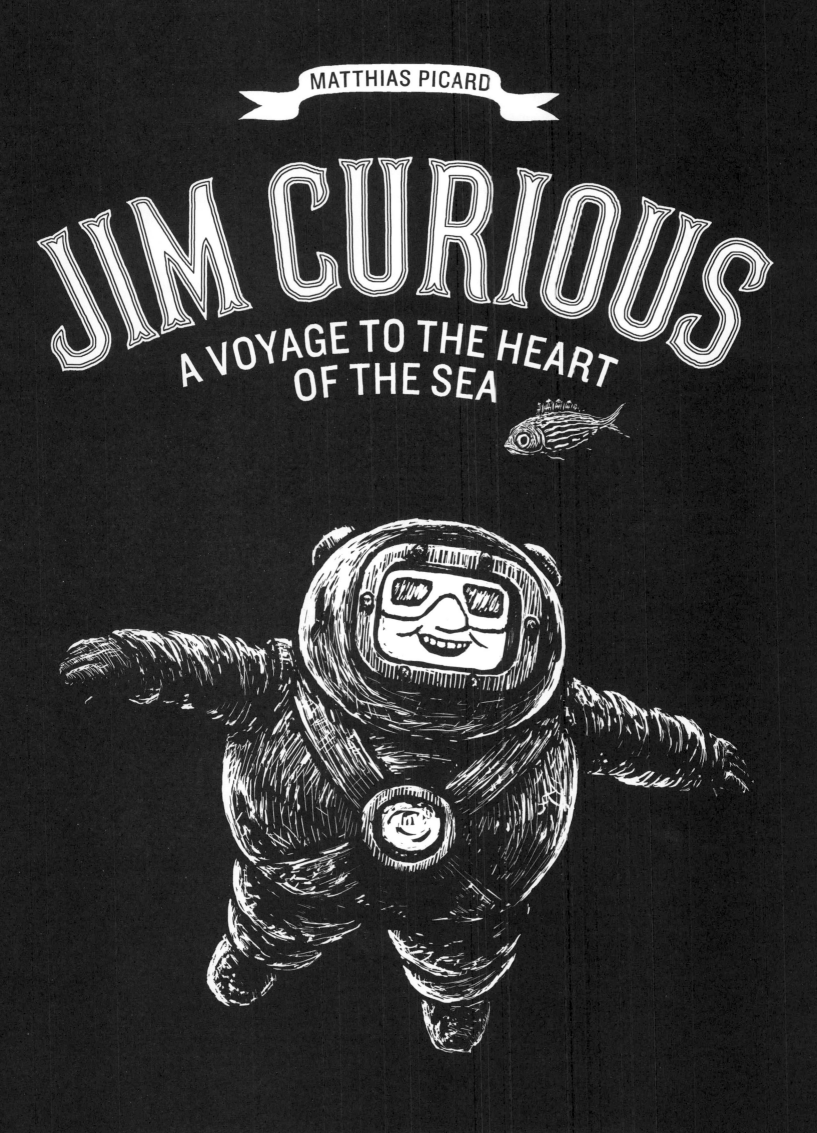

ABRAMS BOOKS FOR YOUNG READERS
NEW YORK

At the back of the book,
there are two pairs of 3-D glasses—
one for you and one for a friend—
that you will need to put on to fully enjoy
Jim Curious. To achieve the best possible
viewing experience, you should avoid
strong direct light on the pages,
which will lessen the 3-D effect.

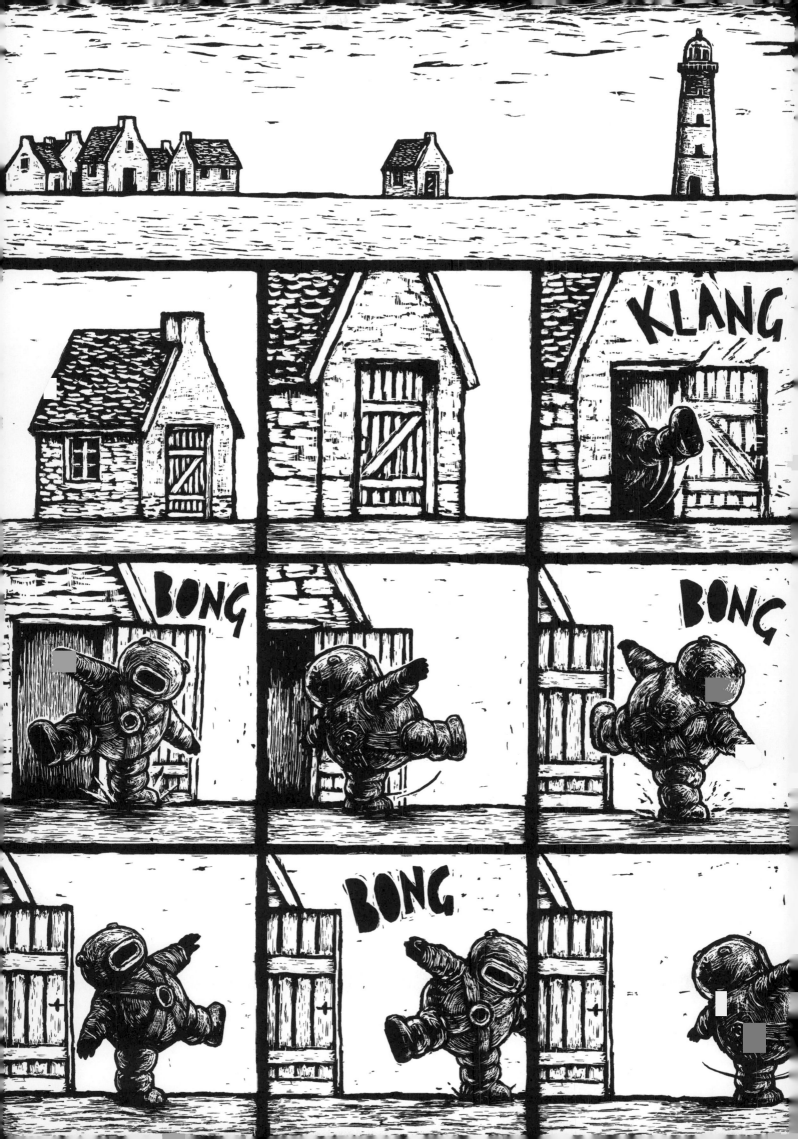

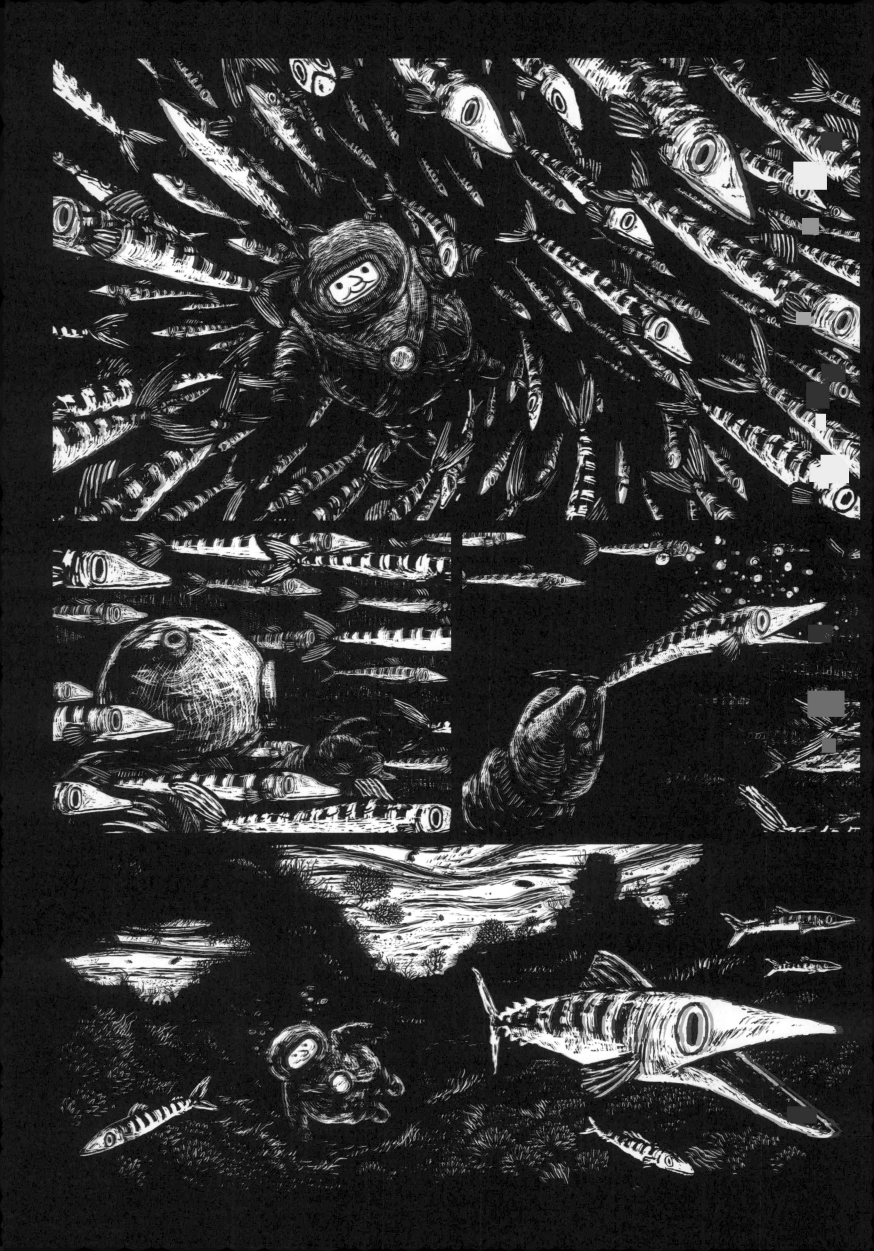

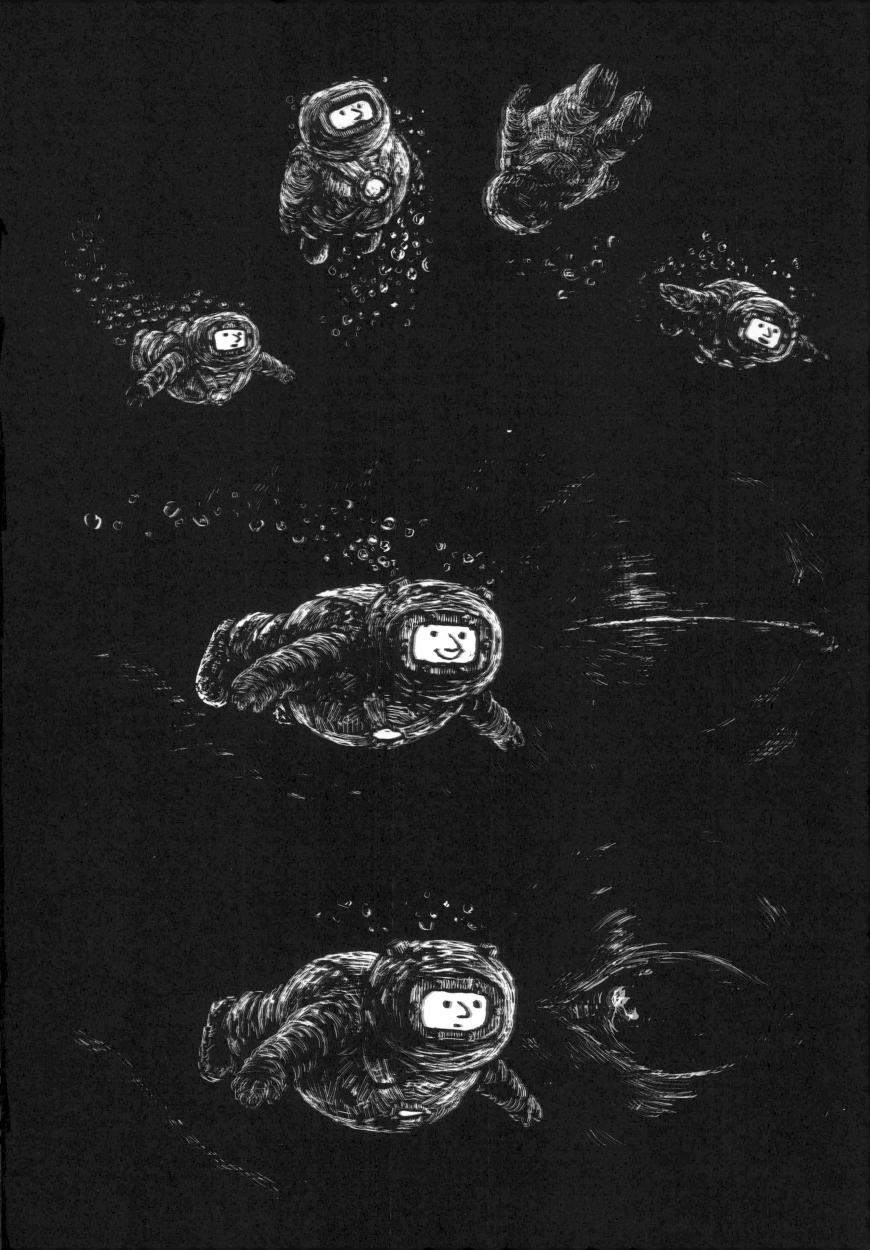

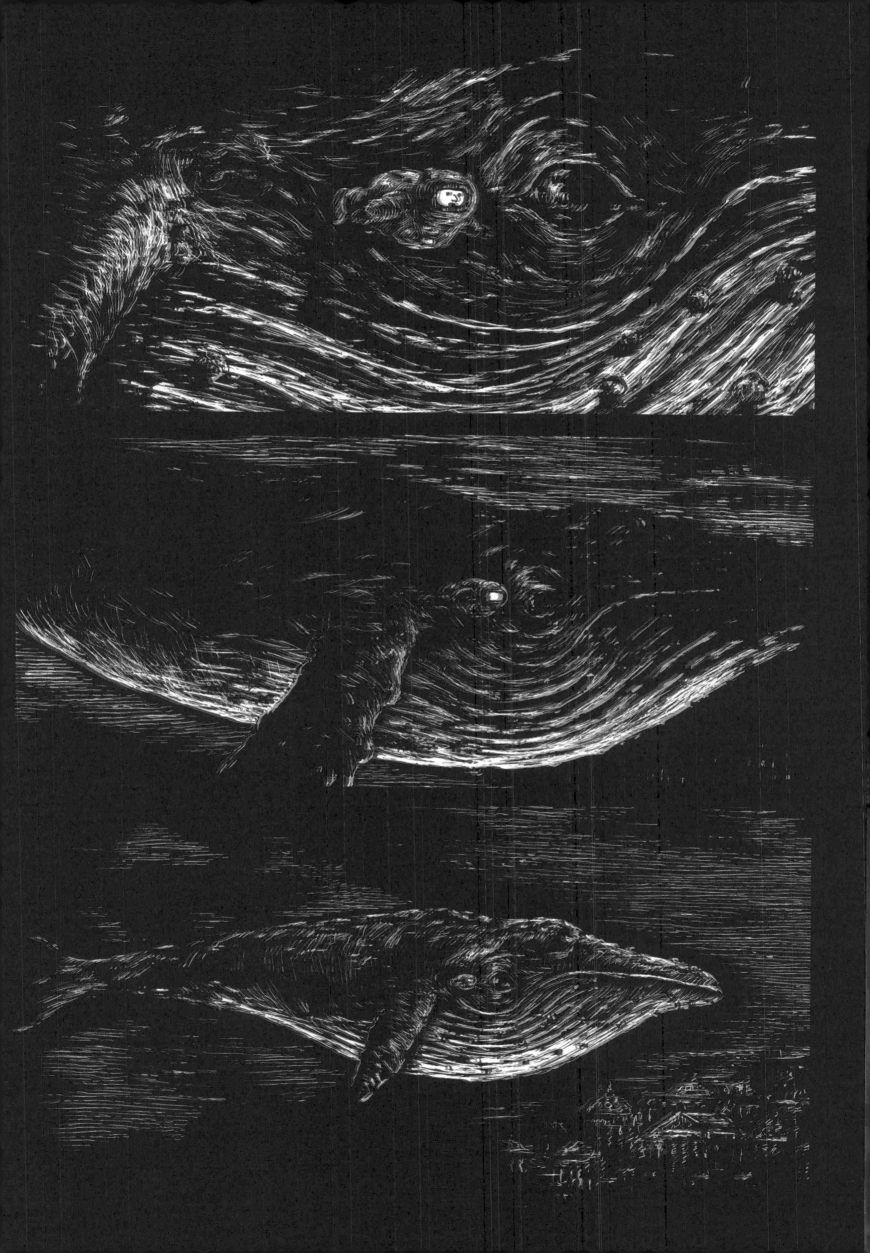

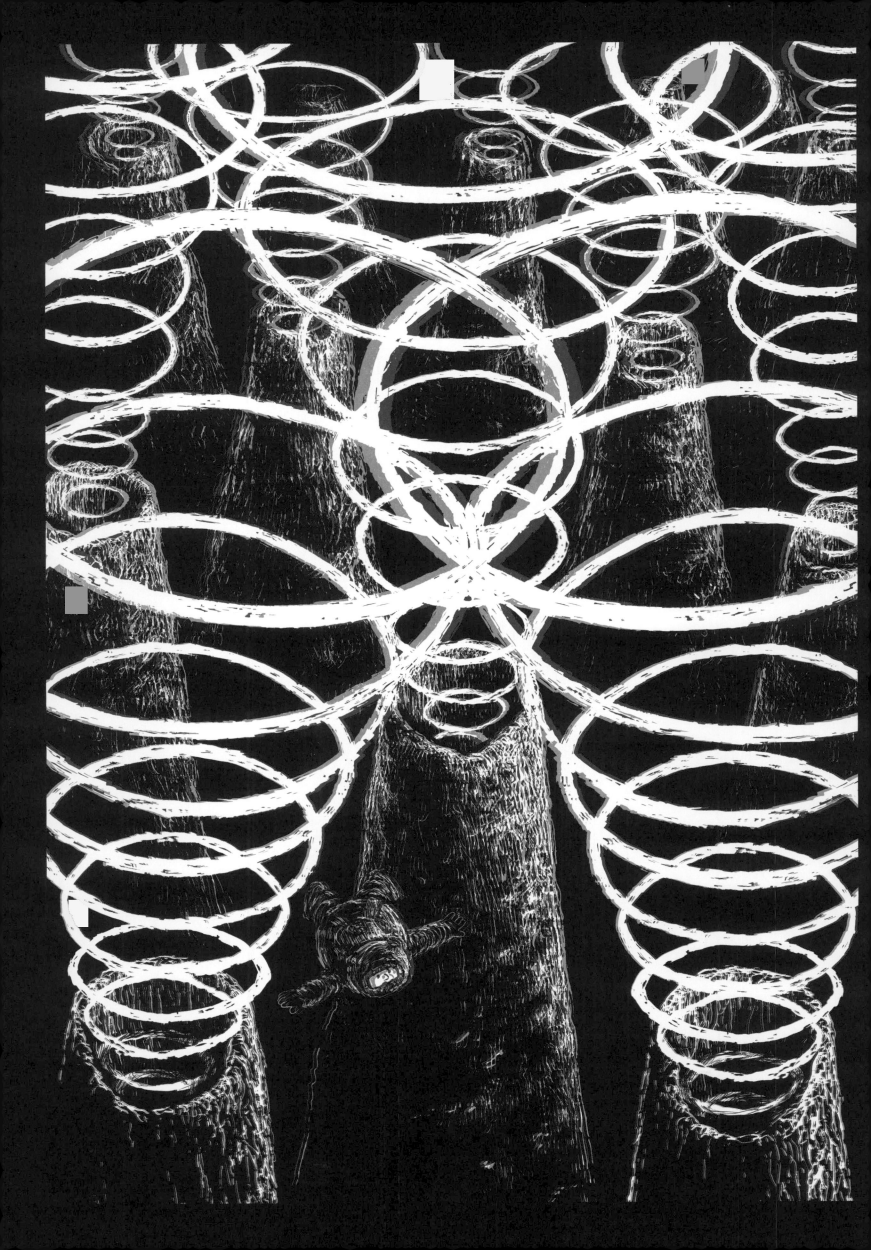

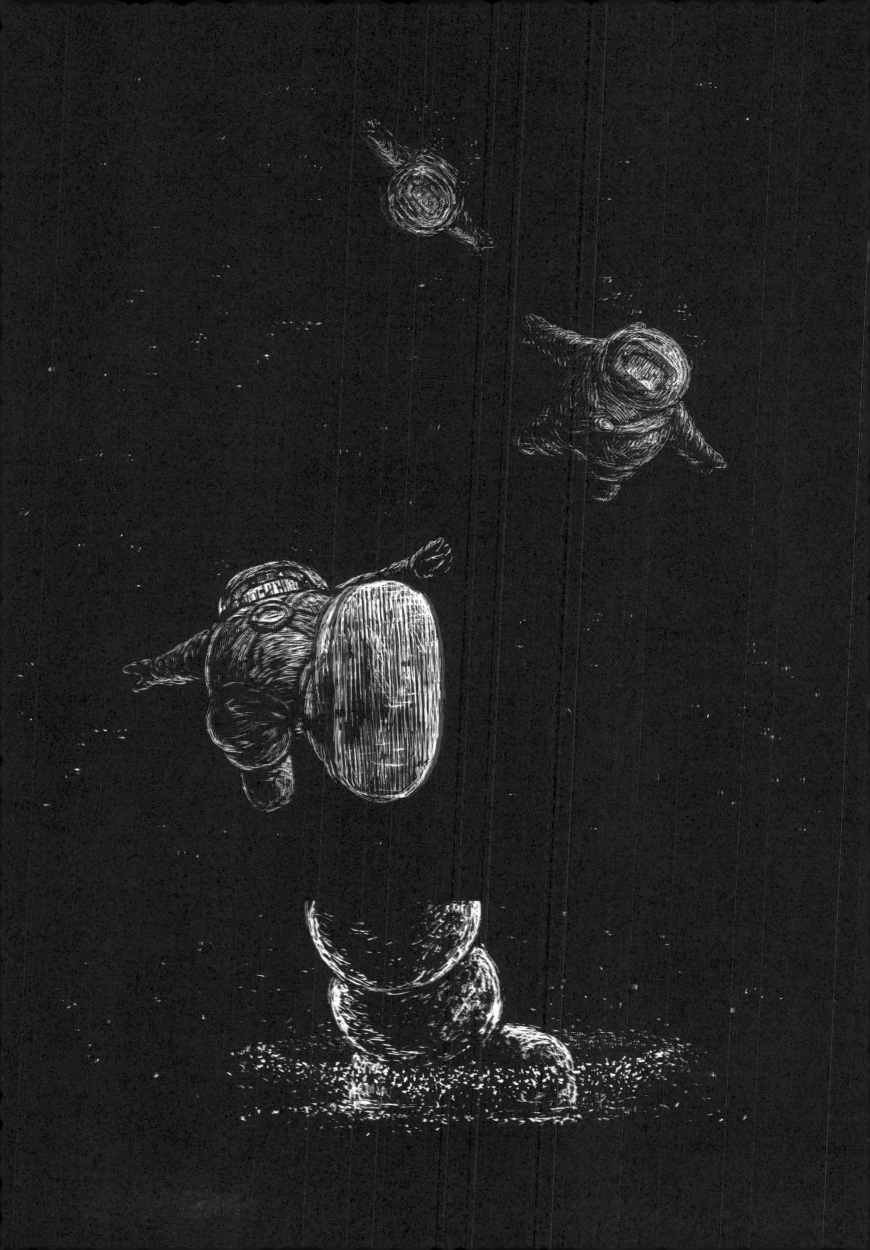

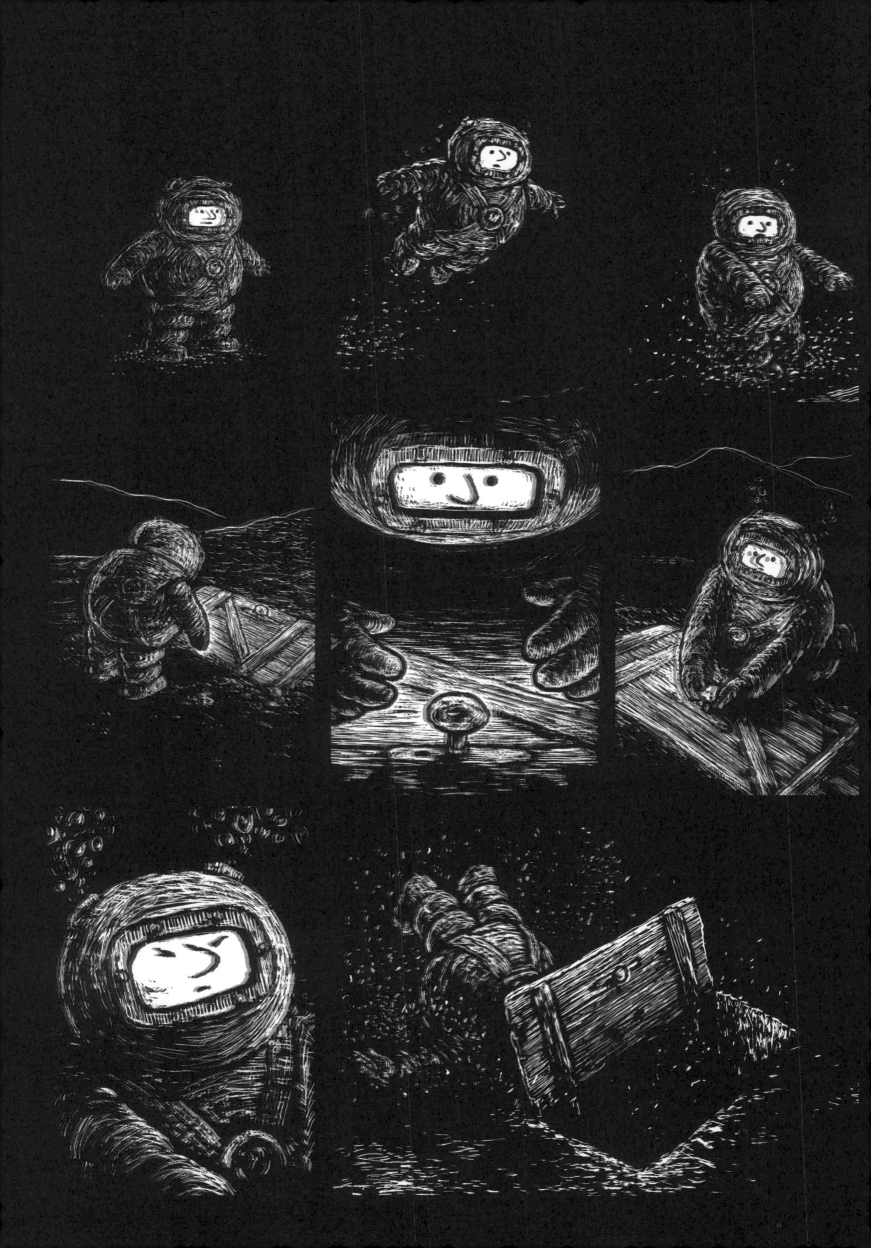

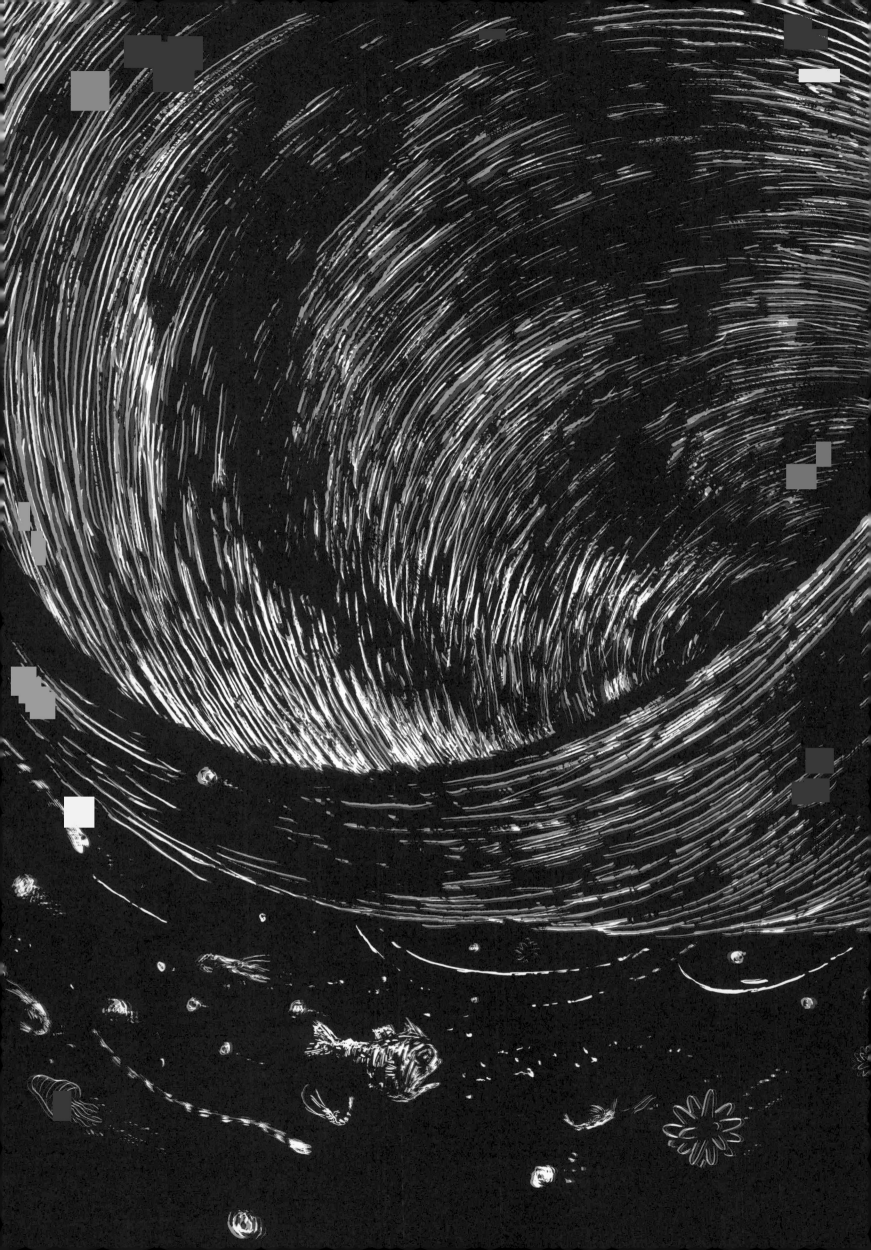

Library of Congress Control Number: 2013941970
ISBN: 978-1-4197-1043-8

Original edition copyright © 2024 & Matthias Picard, Strasbourg, 2012
This edition copyright © Harry N. Abrams, Inc., 2014

Originally published in France by Editions 2024 as *JIM CURIOUS,
Voyage au Coeur de l'Océan*. Rights arranged through Nicolas Grivel Agency.

Printed and bound in China
10 9 8 7 6 5 4 3 2 1

Abrams Books for Young Readers are available at special discounts when
purchased in quantity for premiums and promotions as well as fundraising
or educational use. Special editions can also be created to specification. For
details, contact specialsales@abramsbooks.com or the address below.

ABRAMS
THE ART OF BOOKS SINCE 1949

115 West 18th Street
New York, NY 10011
www.abramsbooks.com